This book may be returned to any Wiltshire
library. To renew this book phone your library
or visit the website: www.wiltshire.gov.uk

Wiltshire Council
Where everybody matters

LM6.108.5

Tilly's Pony Tails
Stripy
the zebra foal

Pippa Funnell

Illustrated by Jennifer Miles

Orion
Children's Books

First published in Great Britain in 2011
by Orion Children's Books
This new edition published in 2013
by Orion Children's Books
An imprint of Hachette Children's Group
Part of Hodder & Stoughton
Carmelite House
50 Victoria Embankment
London EC4Y 0DZ

5 7 9 10 8 6 4

Text copyright © Pippa Funnell MBE 2011, 2013
Illustrations copyright © Jennifer Miles 2011

The right of Pippa Funnell and Jennifer Miles to be identified
as the author and illustrator of this work has been asserted.

A catalogue record for this book is available from the British Library.

ISBN 978 1 4440 0263 8

Printed and bound in the UK by Clays Ltd, St Ives Plc

An Hachette UK Company
www.orionchildrensbooks.com
www.tillysponytails.co.uk

For Caz and Julie, two of my special friends
who joined us on Safari

Hello!

When I was little, I, like Tilly, was absolutely crazy about horses and ponies. All my books, pictures and toys had something to do with my four-legged friends.

I was lucky because a great friend of my mother's lent us a little woolly pony called Pepsi. He lived in the field at my best friend's house. I loved spending as much time as possible with him, but hated having to scrape all the mud off his shaggy winter coat. I used to lie in bed at night longing for the day I'd be able to have a smart horse all clipped and snuggled up in a stable with nice warm rugs.

My birthday treat every year was to go to The Horse of the Year Show, and

I remember going to Badminton and Burghley as a child. It was seeing top riders at these famous venues that gave me the inspiration to follow my dreams.

Now I've had the opportunity to ride some wonderful horses, all of whom have a special place in my heart. It's thanks to them that I have achieved my dreams and won so many competitions at the highest level. I still ride all day, every day, live, sleep and breathe horses and I love every minute of it.

Many of you will not be as used to horses as I am, so I have tried to include some of what I have learned in these books. At the back is a glossary so you can look up any unfamiliar words.

I hope you will enjoy reading the books in my series *Tilly's Pony Tails*, as much as I have enjoyed creating a girl who, like me, follows her passions. I hope that Tilly will inspire many readers to follow their dreams.

Love

One

The leaves and branches glistened with
frost. Tilly Redbrow could hardly feel her
fingers and toes, despite the warm silk boot
liners and fleecy gloves she was wearing,
but she didn't mind. She always enjoyed
winter rides along the forest tracks near
Silver Shoe Farm.

Tilly nudged her horse, Magic Spirit,
with both heels

'Come on, boy!' she said. 'Let's pick up
the pace!'

Immediately Magic moved into a canter. It felt amazing. The trees passed by in a blur and the track disappeared behind them.

When Tilly sensed Magic was tiring, she asked him to slow and then come to a halt. She waited for her brother, Brook, and his stunning black thoroughbred, Solo, to catch up.

'Wow!' said Brook. 'You went for it then! Does Magic have a secret dream to be a racehorse, do you think?'

Tilly laughed.

'Maybe.'

Suddenly she felt her phone buzz from inside her waterproof riding jacket. Unfortunately, she had so many layers on, she couldn't get to it in time.

'Never mind. I'm sure it was just my mum wanting to know what time I need a lift home. I should probably get Magic back to the stables.'

'Okay,' said Brook. 'I've got to go and do some studying anyway. More exams! I wish I could be on holiday right now. I've had enough of school-work.'

'A holiday somewhere hot?' Tilly said, as she breathed warmth onto her finger tips.

'If only,' said Brook. 'Remember how it feels in the summer, to go riding wearing just a t-shirt? All these bulky clothes get in the way.'

Just then, Tilly's phone buzzed again. She managed to get one glove off and undo her zip, but she didn't get to it before it stopped. 'Missed call' read the screen. The number wasn't one she recognised.

'Oh,' she said. 'It's not my mum, after all.'

'Well, whoever it is, they obviously want to talk to you,' said Brook.

Tilly shrugged.

She was about to put the phone away when it began to ring again. This time she answered it.

'Hello?'

'Hi. Is this Tilly Redbrow's phone?'

It was a friendly voice, a young woman.

'Er, yes.'

'I'm calling from *Pony* magazine.'

Tilly gasped and glanced at Brook. She couldn't think what the call was about, but if it was something to do with *Pony* magazine it had to be good.

'A few months ago,' said the woman, 'you sent us a picture of your beautiful

horse, Magic Spirit. It was for our horse safari competition.'

'I remember,' said Tilly, her eyes getting wider.

'Well, I'm really pleased to tell you . . . '

Tilly held her breath.

'What? What is it?'

'You've won!'

'Really?'

'Yes! Congratulations, Tilly! Magic Spirit's photograph was the one drawn out of thousands of entries. You're going on safari. How do you feel?'

'I – I – I don't believe it! It's brilliant!'

Tilly could hardly speak. She waved at Brook and gave a thumbs-up sign. Brook smiled back, but she could tell he had no idea why she was so excited.

'Well, I'll let the good news sink in,' the woman continued, 'then I'll call back later with the details. I'm sure you already know that the trip is for three people. You'll have to take an adult, of course, but you can bring a friend too.'

Tilly didn't need to think about who that would be. As she said goodbye, she knew instantly.

'Who was that then?' Brook asked. 'What's made you so happy?'

'That holiday . . .' said Tilly. It was hard to get the words out. 'The sunny one we were just talking about, away from all your exam stress . . .'

'Yes?'

'Pack your suitcase! We're going!'

'Huh?'

'I've just won a horse safari trip to

Africa! Thanks to *Pony* magazine – and a photograph of Magic Spirit! Do you remember the one I entered ages ago?'

'Wow!' said Brook. 'Thanks! That's amazing! And congratulations! I've always wanted to go on safari. It's a good job you finally got to answer your phone!'

They both laughed, then Tilly leaned forward and gave Magic a hug. She stroked his neck and whispered in his ear.

'Well done, boy. Because of you, or at least, because of a photo of you, I've won a holiday.'

Soothed by Tilly's affectionate touch, Magic gave a nicker.

'I always thought I was lucky to have you in my life. Now, this proves it! I can't wait to tell everyone at Silver Shoe.'

'Come on,' said Brook. 'Let's go.'

Tilly and Brook turned their horses around. They trotted back to the end of the track, then walked up the lane, towards the gates of Silver Shoe Farm. Tilly smiled the whole way.

Two

When they arrived at the yard, Tilly and Brook found their friend, Mia. She was grooming her horse, Autumn Glory. They told her about the trip.

'Huh! I'm so jealous!' said Mia. 'I'll be stuck here in freezing Britain. But, seriously, I'm pleased for you guys. Just don't get eaten by lions!'

'Lions? I hadn't thought about that,' said Brook.

'Of course,' said Tilly. 'We're bound

to see some. It's a safari.'

'Hm,' he said, looking slightly worried. 'I hope our horses can gallop fast.'

After Brook had taken Solo back to Cavendish Hall, the boarding school he attended, Tilly fed Magic and settled him for the night. Then she rushed home to tell her family the exciting news. She found her mum in the kitchen, reading a magazine and sipping tea.

'You won't believe this,' she said, as she kicked off her riding boots.

'Believe what?' said her mum, without looking up.

'Remember that competition I entered last year? The one where I had to send in a photo of Magic?'

'Yes.'

'I've won! We're going on a horse safari to Africa!'

Tilly's mum nearly dropped her cup of tea.

'That's brilliant!' she said, with a gasp.

'Will you come with me?' said Tilly.
'You and Brook?'

She gave her mum a hug.

'Wow, Tilly! Well, we'll have to talk to your dad, but I'd love to!'

They were both so happy and excited that they started laughing.

Tilly's dad came to the kitchen door, with Adam, Tilly's younger brother, bouncing up and down behind him.

'What's all the fuss about?' he said.

'We heard you from upstairs!' said Adam.

Tilly and her mum grinned at one another.

'We're going on a horse safari!'

For the rest of that evening, Tilly and her mum sat at the computer and looked up information about their trip.

'The Okavango Delta, Botswana,' said Tilly, checking the details that the woman at the magazine had emailed her. 'Apparently it's ideal for riding, with vast areas of savannah, desert, and wetlands. We'll get to see loads of wildlife, including elephants and zebras – and lions!'

'It sounds incredible,' said Tilly's mum. 'And I'm so pleased they're able to look after inexperienced riders like me. I'd hate to miss out on the sightseeing.'

'The weather will be hot and dry,' said Tilly. 'Not like it is here at the moment. Hey, look at that . . .'

She pointed to a photograph of a beautiful camp, half-hidden by exotic trees and shrubs. It looked fantastic.

What Tilly was most excited about, however, were the horses. She browsed through several photos and admired the team of handsome bays, glossy chestnuts and stunning greys. She read that they were carefully selected breeds, known for their hardiness and ability to cope in extreme conditions.

'It says here that we'll have our own private guide,' said her mum, 'who'll be able to take us to some of the best wildlife spotting areas.'

'I can't wait,' said Tilly.

The day of the trip finally came. The flight wasn't until the afternoon, so once she'd finished her packing, Tilly wanted to spend her last few hours with Magic. Her dad agreed to drop her at Silver Shoe.

As they drove along the tree-lined lane, through the five-bar gate, and into the yard, Tilly gave a sigh. She was thrilled to be going on safari and though she knew it was only for a week, it still felt as if she was leaving Magic for an eternity.

She saw Angela, Silver Shoe's owner, holding a bag of horse feed, talking to her friends, Mia and Tim. They were standing beside the new stable block, which had been re-built since the terrible fire they'd had at Christmas.

'Hi, guys,' Tilly called, giving them a wave.

'Hey, aren't you off soon?' said Tim.

'Later,' said Tilly. 'I've come to say goodbye to Magic. You'll keep an eye on him, won't you?'

'Yes.'

'You know he doesn't like his drinking water too cold. And when you clean his hooves, he prefers it if you start with the front ones. And . . .'

'Tilly!' said Mia. 'You sound like my mum when she's worried about leaving me home alone for an hour. Don't forget to turn the tap off. Don't forget to lock the windows. Don't forget to unplug the toaster. Honestly. Magic will be fine!'

'He'll be treated like a king,' said Angela.

Tilly nodded

'Thanks everyone. It's just I'm going to miss him so much.'

'I know,' said Angela. 'He'll miss you too. He's down in the long field. Go and see him.'

As soon as Magic saw Tilly coming towards the fence he pricked his ears. She went through the gate and stood in the field with him.

'Hello, gorgeous boy!' she said, wrapping her arms around his neck.

She felt his warm breath.

'Are you looking for a treat?' she asked.

He lowered his head and nuzzled the pocket where she usually kept carrots or mints.

'Nothing in that one today. Try the other side.'

Tilly turned her body slightly and showed him the other one, which held two juicy carrots.

'There you go,' she said, holding them out to him one by one.

'When I'm in Botswana, I'll think about you every day.'

She held his nose and looked into his eyes. He gazed back at her and made a soft wickering sound.

'Now, be good while I'm away,' she said gently. 'Don't give Angela and the others too much trouble. I'll be home next week and we'll go for lots of lovely long hacks, I promise.'

Tilly kissed Magic's nose and walked away. She knew she had to keep going. She tried her best to look forward, but couldn't resist glancing back briefly. Saying goodbye to Magic was always so hard.

Three

Going to the airport was very exciting.
Brook had taken a taxi over to the
Redbrow house and then Tilly's dad drove
them all together. Tilly's little brother,
Adam, came too. He didn't want to miss
the fun. The journey seemed to take
forever, but finally they approached the
airport car park, and Tilly could see the
lights of the planes taking off and coming
into land.

'That'll be us soon,' said Brook.

'Africa here we come,' said Tilly, and she squeezed his arm.

They said goodbye to Mr Redbrow and Adam and went straight to the check-in desk.

'I hope we haven't brought too much luggage,' said Tilly's mum. 'They said we had to keep things to a minimum.'

She glanced at Tilly's suitcase then at Brook's.

'You know, Tilly wanted to bring every pair of jodhpurs and riding boots she owns!'

Brook shrugged and gave a small, embarrassed nod. Tilly guessed he'd probably done the same.

They were quickly through check-in and by the time they'd browsed in the shops, and bought their sun cream and mosquito repellent, it was time to board the plane.

'Goodbye, cold, rainy England!' said Tilly, as they climbed the steps to the cabin. 'And hello, sunshine!'

'It's going to be weird going from winter to summer in only fourteen hours,' said Brook.

They made themselves comfortable on the plane and decided the best thing to do was to get some sleep. They wanted to be as refreshed as possible for the start of their trip.

For Tilly, sleep didn't come easily. Her mind was full of her first long haul flight, and arriving in Botswana. She wondered what it would be like. She remembered some of the horses she'd seen in the photographs and the beautiful backdrop of the African bush.

She took out a copy of her favourite book, *Black Beauty*. She'd read it so many times, but she always loved re-reading it. She only managed two chapters, however, before her eyelids began to grow heavy.

Tilly rubbed the sleep from her eyes. Her mum checked their itinerary.

'Once we get through passport control,' she said, reading from the *Pony* magazine information pack, 'we have to get a connecting internal flight on a smaller plane. What an adventure!'

At last the plane landed. When it stopped, everyone stood up, stretched, and retrieved their luggage from the overhead lockers. Slowly, with help from the flight attendants, they made their way down the aisles to the exits.

'Thank you for flying with us,' said one of the attendants, as Tilly walked past. 'Have a great trip!'

'Thanks,' said Tilly. 'We will!'

Then, finally, she took her first breath of African air. Stepping onto the tarmac, everything felt different. The sky was brilliant blue and there was a sweet, floral smell drifting through the heat.

'It's a good job we've brought plenty of sun cream,' said Tilly's mum. 'It's so hot!'

Tilly didn't say anything. She was too busy taking it all in.

They collected their luggage, had their passports checked, then walked through to the arrivals gate. A young man was waiting for them. He was dressed in khaki safari gear and held a sign which read:

'Welcome, Tilly Redbrow and Co.'

He saw them and stepped forward, with a friendly smile.

'Dumela! You must be Tilly! My name's Zolano. I'm very pleased to meet you. My job is to help you get to the small

plane that will fly you to the bush – there are no roads, you see, and it would take around five hours by jeep. But there's a small landing strip nearby where you will be met by members of the camp.'

The three of them introduced themselves and shook Zolano's hand.

'We really are going into the middle of nowhere!' said Tilly, smiling at Brook.

'Yes,' said Zolano. 'It will be very different from what you're used to. There are no shops or anything like that, and apart from the camp, you'll be as close to nature as you ever will be.'

Tilly and her mum felt a little uneasy when they saw the size of the plane that was to take them on the last leg of their journey.

'Cool,' said Brook. 'I've never been on a plane that only carries fourteen passengers.'

'If you like, you two can sit at the front just behind the pilot and his co-pilot,' Zolano said to Brook and Tilly, with a wink.

Tilly's mum opted to sit at the back. Tilly thought she looked a bit pale. The seats between them were filled with other people who would be making up the rest of their safari group.

'Wow! Look at all those buttons and lights and gauges,' said Brook.

The co-pilot, Dave, was from South Africa, and he was explaining the control panel to Brook as they waited for the pilot.

'Maybe I don't want to be a champion eventer any more – being a pilot could be just as thrilling.' Brook could hardly contain his enthusiasm.

'Boys and their toys,' said Tilly, nudging Brook.

The forty-five minute flight was incredible, and the views were spectacular. Even Tilly's mum relaxed, despite the slightly bumpy ride. Dave pointed out a large herd of elephants. Tilly tingled with excitement when she spotted the small grey dots below them, not quite believing she was actually seeing them.

At last, the plane began to descend towards a small landing strip in the middle of the bush. It gradually came to a halt, and there waiting for them were two safari jeeps, with four very welcoming members from the camp.

One of them stepped forward as

everyone got off the plane.

'My name is John,' he said, with a warm smile. 'And funnily enough, people tend to call me "Safari John".'

Safari John, who Tilly thought must be the one in charge, then introduced Sekongo, Bongwi and Helen.

'Sekongo and Bongwi will be your guides for the week, and Helen is sort of the camp "housekeeper" – a "campkeeper", in fact!'

After all the introductions, and having loaded their luggage into the jeeps, everyone climbed into the open-sided vehicles and then they were on their way to base camp!

Tilly liked Sekongo instantly. He seemed full of energy and his broad smile and bright, keen eyes lit up his face when he talked. He carried their luggage without any effort. She walked beside him.

'What does "dumela" mean?' she asked. 'Zolano used it when he met us at the airport.'

'Dumela,' he explained. 'It's Setswana for "hello". Setswana is the national language of Botswana. You'll hear it a lot while you're on safari. Do you like zebras?'

'Yes.'

'Giraffes?'

'Yes.'

'Lions.'

'Yes.'

'So you're an animal lover?'

'Definitely,' said Tilly. 'I love all animals, but I like horses the most.'

'Ah. Wonderful creatures! You'll have a truly remarkable time while you're on horse safari. Many of our guests say it's the best riding they've ever done. They come back year after year. There's nothing like it. Did you know zebras are a close relative of horses? Although unlike horses, they've never been domesticated. There have been many attempts to train them for riding, but they're too unpredictable and they tend to panic under stress. But they have amazing stamina, and when they're chased, they'll zigzag from side-to-side, so it's difficult for predators to catch them.'

'You know a lot about zebras,' said Tilly, fascinated.

'It's my job to know. Any questions, just ask Sekongo!'

'Do you think we'll see any?'

'I'll make sure of it,' he said, and gave her another of his bright smiles.

Four

The journey to the camp took an hour.
There were no roads, just bumpy sand
tracks that had been made by the jeeps.
Tilly was amazed at how far they were
from normal life.

The sky seemed huge, somehow bigger
than it did in England. She wished she
could show it to Magic. She knew he'd
love all the open space and freedom. She
imagined galloping him across it, alongside
the safari horses. Every now and again she

glanced at Brook and smiled. He gave her a friendly nudge

'We're actually here,' he whispered.

Tilly giggled.

'I know. I can't believe it!'

Tilly's mum sat in the front of the jeep, next to Sekongo. They talked about what they were going to do.

'When we get there, we'll have some lunch,' said Safari John, who was sitting next to Tilly and Brook. 'Then you'll meet the horses and tomorrow morning we'll get up early and go for our first game ride.'

'What's a game ride?'

'Wildlife spotting by horse. We'll trek into the bush and hopefully we'll get to see some animal action.'

'What will we see?' said Tilly.

'All sorts. I've already told you about the zebras. There's been a large herd spotted recently. I also know a very special place where we might see hippos. There'll be plenty of okapi, monkeys and birds. And we might even get to see the big cats. Last week, a lion pride was spotted in the area.'

'I hope they're not hungry lions,' said Brook, looking nervous.

'Don't worry,' said Sekongo. 'I will do everything I can to keep you safe. We won't take any unnecessary risks.'

Finally, the jeep drove over a rickety man-made bridge and they entered the camp. They were surrounded by lush forest.

'You'll feel as though you're really in the wilds out here,' said Sekongo. 'But it's very comfortable. We even have eco-showers and toilets. Water is pumped fresh from a nearby spring. Everything gets recycled. Nothing is wasted. We have to respect our wonderful Mother Nature.'

Tilly nodded. This made sense to her. Since joining Silver Shoe Farm, she'd learned to love the surrounding countryside. It wasn't as impressive as the African Bush, but it was beautiful in its way. And it deserved to be looked after.

'Okay,' said Sekongo. 'I'll show you around, then you'll be taken to your tent.'

'Tents?'

'Oh yes. It's all tents here apart from the barn where the horses are kept. But rest assured, they are much nicer than the tents you'd put up in your garden at home!'

Tilly and Brook looked at each other. 'How cool is that?'

'You'll be very close to nature. You'll get to see all kinds of birds, monkeys and insects from the comfort of your rooms!'

'Uh oh!' said Tilly's mum. 'I'm not a fan of insects.'

'If you see anything that worries you,' said Sekongo, his eyes twinkling, 'just call for me.'

When they got to their tent, they saw it was a tent like no other. It was set on a concrete floor and had a wooden veranda outside. It was huge. It even had its own bathroom.

They went inside.

'Wow! It's nothing like I imagined,' said Tilly's mum.

It had separate bedroom compartments and was open on both sides, so it looked out onto the trees and exotic flowers. The bathroom area didn't have a roof.

'We can have star-lit showers. How lovely!'

In the middle of the tent, on a wooden table, Tilly noticed a large basket of fresh fruit.

'I guess that's for us.'

She picked out a banana and began to peel it. Then she saw an envelope resting behind the basket.

For Tilly Redbrow.

She tore it open and found a large congratulations card enclosed. It had a photograph of Magic Spirit on the front, the one that had been picked in the competition prize draw. Sure enough, the card was from the magazine.

Dear Tilly,

We hope you really enjoy your trip. Congratulations once again on winning. Have a great time!

From everyone at *Pony* magazine

She held the card to her chest. She felt so special. And it was extra nice to see that photo of Magic again. She propped it up on the table. It made it feel almost as though he was in the room with her.

She went outside and found Brook lying in a hammock. He was swinging gently. She climbed in next to him.

'Ah, this is the life,' he said. 'No worrying about exams for me while I'm here!'

'Bliss!' said Tilly, watching the trees, her arms dangling over the sides of the hammock. 'It would be good to relax in one of these after a long, tiring day at the stables. I can't wait for our game ride tomorrow.'

'I've got a feeling this is going to be a great trip,' said Brook.

Five

After a short rest, Tilly, her mum, and
Brook were invited for some lunch. The
main tent was busy with other guests and
there was lots of conversation about riding
and wildlife spotting. Tilly listened eagerly.

There was a delicious array of food and
they could help themselves. There were
trays of fresh fruit – kiwis, pineapples,
melons, guavas, coconuts and other things
Tilly didn't even recognise. And there were
all kinds of breads and grilled meats.

As she filled her plate and made herself a cocktail of fresh juice, one of the guests introduced himself.

'My name is Peter Melesi,' he said. 'I'm a ranger at a nearby game reserve, but I come here whenever I can. I'm a good friend of John's and I love the riding safaris here. Horseback is one of the most exciting ways to see this countryside.'

When they'd finished eating, Sekongo and Bongwi took them to meet their horses. Peter Melesi came too, along with several other guests.

The stable area was at the back of the camp. One by one they were introduced to the horses, which had been matched to them according to size and riding experience.

'Here is your horse, Tilly,' said Sekongo.

Tilly's stomach flipped with excitement as he led her over to a statuesque chestnut with a white snip and socks.

'Do you think you can manage him?'

The horse was bigger than Magic, but Tilly wasn't put off.

'Definitely. He's about 16.2hh, right?'

'Yes,' said Sekongo, looking surprised. 'His name is Olorato. He's seven years old and he loves life, although he can be a bit of a dawdler. He often likes to stop and have a munch on the plant-life, but I think you've got enough experience to know how to keep him moving. Just be firm with the leg.'

Tilly held her hand to Olorato's nose.

'Hello, boy,' she said.

He prodded her palm and sniffed her horsehair bracelets.

'So, you and I are going to be partners for a few days. Pleased to meet you!'

Olorato lowered his eyelids and blew gently through his nose. Tilly patted his shoulder and then looked round to see the other horses.

Brook had been given a dark bay gelding called Kaylar, and Tilly's mum, who was a beginner, would ride a responsible, calm buckskin mare called Nayang. She was going to be led by another guide, as were some of the other less experienced riders.

'Strange names,' said Tilly.

'They are all popular Botswanian names,' said Sekongo.

Next day, everyone got up early to greet their horses before heading off. There was no grooming or mucking out to be done. The camp stable hands did this for them.

'Now it really feels like a holiday,' said Brook.

As they walked to the stables, baboons were making bizarre calls to each other across the tree canopy.

Tilly and Brook giggled. They couldn't believe some of the strange noises they were hearing.

'It's a bit more interesting than the usual sound of pigeons and stray cats, eh!' said Tilly's mum.

Sekongo looked up.

'It's perfect weather for a riding safari,' he said. 'The sun will rise in about ten minutes and we'll have clear blue skies. Okay, everyone, let's get going.'

Tilly mounted Olorato. He was slightly bigger than Magic, but had a similar build. He was very responsive, although just as Sekongo had warned, as soon as they began to move, he stopped and plunged his nose into a nearby shrub. She pulled him up sharply and he carried on.

'We'll have no dawdling today, thank you!' she said, in a firm but affectionate voice.

Some of the other guests had joined them for the day's riding. Sekongo rode out in front and the others followed in a line down a dirt track.

Tilly's mum was right behind, with several other beginner riders, who all had their own guides. Tilly and Brook, because of their experience, were allowed to ride at the back with Peter Melesi.

As Tilly urged Olorato on, she grinned up at Brook. She felt as if she was going to burst with excitement. They'd only just left the camp and it already felt like an adventure.

As the track widened, they were able to ride side-by-side. Peter Melesi joined them.

'Beautiful, isn't it?' he said, breathing in deeply as he patted his grey mare.

Tilly couldn't help noticing that Sekongo was carrying a gun: a black rifle.

'What's the gun for?' she said.

'Oh, don't worry,' said Peter. 'It's an essential part of a ranger's equipment. Remember, a horse is prey for a lion. The gun provides protection. If it has to be used, it's to keep you and your horse safe.'

'Do you think we'll see lions today?' said Brook.

'If we do, I'm afraid we'll have to quietly retreat. We tend to go looking for lions when we're in the jeeps. It's too dangerous with the horses.'

Tilly liked the idea of lions, but the animal she most wanted to catch a glimpse of, after hearing Sekongo's explanation about how they were related to horses, was the zebra. She looked across the horizon and kept an eye out for those distinctive black and white stripes.

It wasn't long before streaks of orange-red light began to split the sky. The clouds dispersed and the sun rose in full.

'Drink plenty of water,' warned Sekongo. 'We'll have little protection from the heat out here. You have all got water bottles attached to the front of your saddles.'

Eventually they left the track and took off into the open scrubland. The terrain was rough but the horses could handle it. When it was safe, Sekongo gave some of the more experienced riders the opportunity to canter. Tilly could tell Olorato was keen to stretch his legs so she encouraged him forward. With the heat and dust and vast, open space, it was exhilarating.

Suddenly, she heard Sekongo asking everyone to stop.

'Hey!' he whispered. 'Look to your right, just by the mud-hole. Can you see? There's a rhinoceros having his breakfast.'

They all turned and gasped as they spotted the majestic rhino in front of them. He was munching grass peacefully, coated up to his shoulders in dried mud.

'Wow!' said Tilly.

'It's amazing,' said Tilly's mum. 'I can't believe we're this close. What's that on his head?'

She pointed to a little brown bird with a red beak, which seemed to be whispering into the rhino's ear.

'That is an ox-pecker,' said Sekongo. 'He's picking out ticks and mites.'

Just as they were getting used to the sight of the rhino, two tiny antelopes crossed their path.

'Ah. We call them impala,' said Sekongo. 'If we're lucky they'll pose for a photograph.'

Sure enough, the antelopes stopped and gazed at the safari group with their gentle brown eyes and long lashes. Brook and Tilly pulled their cameras from their backpacks and took several photos. The antelopes were sweet, but Tilly was still hoping to see zebras.

They rode on a little further, then stopped near a large water hole and dismounted.

'Yuck,' whispered Brook. 'What's that smell?'

'It's not very nice, whatever it is,' said Tilly's mum.

'Some kind of animal carcass, I think,' said Sekongo. 'I want to see if I can spot some lion tracks. This is an area where they've been seen.'

With his rifle on his back, he passed his horse's reins to another guide, and bent down to the ground. Tilly watched in fascination as he studied the dirt. Then he looked up.

'There's definitely been recent activity,' he said. 'I can see tracks. They've been here for a few days.'

Tilly felt her heart beat faster. The idea of being so close to a ferocious animal was thrilling, but also slightly frightening. She smiled nervously at Brook. He was about to take a photo of her when Tilly's mum cried out.

'Look over there!'

To Tilly's surprise and delight, she saw a herd of zebras in the distance. Their manes were short and stiff and their strange, geometric coats were mesmerising.

Just as the antelopes had done, they stopped for a moment to stare at the horses and people.

Brook lifted his camera again, but Tilly was too absorbed in the sight to worry about taking pictures. As she watched, she imagined she and Magic parading among them, Magic's soft grey coat camouflaged by a sea of black and white stripes.

Then the zebras were on the move, heading across the plain. All that remained of their presence were hoof marks in the ground.

Suddenly, there was a rustling noise from the bush behind them.

Six

'Stay very quiet,' said Sekongo.

He went to investigate.

The rest of the group gathered together and waited, until eventually Sekongo reappeared.

'I've found something,' he said. 'It explains the bad smell. It's interesting. You might want to come and look, but I warn you, if you have a weak stomach, it's not a pretty a sight.'

'What is it?' said Brook.

'A zebra carcass, which confirms we've had lion activity in the area. It's a fairly recent kill so we'll have to be careful. Though it doesn't look as though they'll be coming back to it. They've pretty much stripped it to the bone.'

Tilly winced.

Everyone in the group, including Brook and Tilly's mum, stepped forward, but Tilly hesitated. She could feel tears welling up. The thought of seeing a dead zebra was horrible. She knew it was different in the wild. It wasn't as if one of the horses from Silver Shoe had been attacked by lions, but still, it made her feel sad.

'Aren't you coming?' said Brook.

'I don't know if I want to see this,' she said.

Her mum gave her a reassuring hug.

'You don't have to look, Tilly,' said Sekongo. 'But remember, this is Nature's kingdom, a world of predators and prey. We have to be brave and recognise that Nature has her own laws. A dead zebra means a lion pride has food for a few days. It's all about survival.'

He held out his hand. Slowly, she took it and walked with him. There, in the shade of a tree, was the zebra carcass.

It was lying on its side. Close up, the smell was even worse and there were flies buzzing everywhere. But Sekongo was right. Somehow, it didn't look like a zebra any more. It was a meal, part of the food chain.

Brook, Tilly and her mum stared.

'How long do you think it's been there, Sekongo?' said one of the other members of their group.

'Two days, at least. Now the lions have had their fill, the vultures will find it and take the last of the meat. Looks like an adult female.'

As they turned to go back to their horses, they heard a rustling sound from the bush again.

'What *is* that?' whispered Tilly's mum. 'It's not lions, is it?'

Sekongo shook his head.

'No. Maybe just another impala.'

Nonetheless, he placed his hands on his rifle.

Tilly and the others returned to the horses, who had been waiting quietly with the guides. Everyone was nervous. No one said a word. As she was getting ready to mount, however, Tilly looked back over her shoulder and saw an amazing sight.

Wobbling towards her, on spindly, unsteady legs, was a little zebra foal. Sekongo was crouched behind him, his hands no longer gripping his gun.

Tilly's heart did a somersault. She handed Olarato's rein to Brook and stepped towards them.

'Don't get too close,' said Sekongo, when he saw her approach.

The zebra foal stared at Tilly. Its big velvety eyes looked sad and lost. Hardly aware of what she was doing, Tilly held out her hand and the foal stumbled towards her. It let out a little cry.

'Poor thing,' she whispered. 'Are you looking for your mum? I think the herd went that way.'

She pointed to where the zebras had crossed the plain. There was no sign of them now. The zebra foal gave another small cry.

'I'm afraid,' said Sekongo, 'that this little baby has been left behind.'

'Why? Where's its mother?' said Tilly.

Sekongo looked down at the ground and lowered his eyelids. He nodded towards the zebra carcass.

'Oh,' said Tilly, suddenly realising.

She looked at the carcass, then back at the foal.

'No mother. No family,' she said.

The foal continued to look at her. She had an urge to bundle it up in her arms and give it a big hug. Its head and body looked out of proportion with its legs. Its coat was still fluffy, like Lucky Chance's, the foal born at Silver Shoe, had been.

'We have to leave,' said Sekongo.

'What?'

'We have to leave the foal here,' he repeated.

'But we can't. How will it survive?' said Tilly, a lump in her throat.

Sekongo gave a reluctant shrug.

'It's the way of nature, Tilly. We shouldn't interfere. I know it's hard.'

'But . . .'

Now the lump in Tilly's throat was becoming a sob. The thought of leaving the foal behind to fend for itself when it was so vulnerable and helpless was heartbreaking, even if it was the right thing to do.

'Come now,' said Sekongo. 'Let's go.'

He took her hand again, and slowly they walked back to their horses. To Tilly, it was a walk that seemed to go on forever.

Seven

As they were about to mount, they heard another cry.

'Hey,' said Peter Melesi. He'd been waiting on his horse. 'You're being followed.'

Tilly and Sekongo turned to see that the zebra foal had stepped out of the bush behind them. It was standing a little way from the group, staring and calling. Tilly's spirits lifted. She could see from the smile on Sekongo's face that there was a possibility she might be able to get him to change his mind about helping the foal.

Sekongo scratched his head and looked at Tilly.

'It needs us,' she said. 'Please! Can't we at least take it somewhere safe, away from the lions?'

Peter Melesi walked his horse forward.

'Unfortunately there isn't anywhere in the bush that's safe from lions. Especially

not for a defenceless little foal like this one,' he said. 'But I have an idea. Perhaps we could take the foal to the game reserve where I work. We have a zebra herd there and we have lots of experience in rehabilitating abandoned or injured animals. What do you think, Sekongo?'

Sekongo thought for a minute, then he nodded.

'It's a good plan.'

Tilly grinned.

'Sekongo,' said Peter, 'why don't you make contact with the camp and see if they can send a jeep? I suspect my team won't be able to pick him up straightaway.'

While Peter and Sekongo organised the rescue mission, Tilly, Brook, and the rest of the group watched the foal. At first they didn't get too close, because they didn't want to intimidate it. Then the foal took a few steps towards them.

'Good news,' said Peter, coming over. 'The reserve is happy to take this little one. They're coming to pick him up later.

In the meantime, the camp is sending a jeep to collect him and take him back there.'

'We'll stop for an early lunch,' said Sekongo. 'Once the zebra is safely loaded onto the jeep, we can continue with our safari.'

'Don't worry, stripy boy,' said Tilly. 'We'll look after you.'

On instinct she held out her hand, something she would have done with a horse or foal at Silver Shoe Farm, to allow them to explore and get used to her scent. She never expected the zebra foal to respond. But he lifted his grey nose and sniffed her hand and wrist. He even tried to nibble her horsehair bracelets, just as Magic and some of the other special horses she'd met liked to do.

Tilly could hardly believe that a wild animal in the middle of the African bush was making such bold, physical contact with her. It felt amazing. Tilly's mum held out her hand too. She reached for the foal but he backed away.

'Oh,' said her mum. 'He doesn't seem to like me.'

'Maybe he senses you're not so familiar with horses,' said Brook. 'Let me try.'

He crouched in front of the foal. The zebra was more interested this time, and sniffed Brook's hand, but then he backed off again.

'So it is you,' said Brook, standing up and patting Tilly's shoulder.

Tilly shrugged and smiled. She couldn't help feeling pleased.

'I think you have a magic touch,' said Sekongo.

'She does,' said her mum proudly. 'You should see how well she gets on with her horse, Magic Spirit. It's as if they were made for each other.'

Tilly thought of Magic now. She wondered what he was up to and what he'd make of Stripy the zebra foal. She hoped he wasn't missing her too much, but she knew he'd be well looked after by Mia, Angela and Duncan. She wished she had her phone with her so she could text her friends, but in the middle of the Okavango Delta, unsurprisingly, there was no signal, and she needed a special satellite phone like Sekongo had.

The jeep arrived. Peter and the driver opened the back of the vehicle and pulled down a step. Sekongo encouraged the foal towards it and the other ranger lifted him inside. He didn't seem afraid, even though he'd probably never been in a jeep before, or so near to humans.

'Come on, Stripy,' said Tilly. 'Come on, little one.'

'Are you sure his name is Stripy?' said Brook, with a smile.

'Suits him, don't you think?'

'It certainly does!' said Sekongo.

When the safari group finally got back to the camp, Safari John came out to the stables to greet them.

'So, thanks to you, we have a special guest,' he said, smiling.

Tilly could tell John was an animal lover. He seemed genuinely pleased to have a zebra at his camp.

'He's settled in well, although it will only be a short stay. The team from the game reserve are on their way. We've organised for our vet to get some milk and sterilised bottles and we've set up a little safe area in the grounds, in a quiet spot behind the tents.'

'Can we see him?' said Tilly.

'Of course,' said John. 'Sekongo explained on the phone that you'd somehow charmed this wild zebra foal. That is very special!'

He led Tilly, Brook and her mum to the enclosure. It was a pleasant, comfortable space, away from the noise and activity of the main tent.

Stripy was there. Tilly thought he looked slightly confused, but perfectly happy. He saw Tilly and pricked his ears.

Eight

Tilly and Brook stayed to watch Stripy in his temporary pen, while Tilly's mum went for a swim with some of the other guests in a nearby spring.

'It's been a long, hot and dusty day,' she said. 'Time to cool down.'

'We'll join you later,' said Tilly.

She was looking forward to splashing in the spring herself, but right now, she wanted to make sure that Stripy was okay.

'Maybe you'd like to give him some

milk,' said Ade, the camp vet. 'I've
mixed up a formula which contains all
the vitamins he needs. Normally he'd
be getting milk from his mother, but the
bottle is the next best thing, as he has a
natural sucking reflex. We don't want him
to get too used to interacting with humans,
because it will make it harder for him to
survive. But for now, our priority is to get
something in his tummy. We don't know
how long it's been since he last ate.'

'Do you think he's malnourished?'
asked Brook.

'No, he looks pretty healthy. He's
still very young though. At this stage, it's
feeding around the clock.'

'I don't mind,' said Tilly.

'Kind of you to offer, but you're on
holiday! Anyway, the team from the game
reserve will be taking over soon. Here. You
can help now. Take the bottle and check
the flow.'

Tilly climbed into the pen. Brook stood
at the side and watched. She held the

bottle upside down and tested the milk on the back of her hand. She could feel it was warm, body-temperature. On Ade's instruction, she kneeled beside Stripy and offered him the bottle. She held it near his mouth, at shoulder height.

He wasn't sure at first.

'Give it a tiny shake,' said Ade. 'Let a few drops touch his lips, so he knows what it is.'

When Tilly did this, Stripy seemed to get the idea. He pulled the teat into his mouth and began to suckle. She could feel the bottle pulling in and out of her hand with each mouthful.

'He's hungry!' she said.

Looking down at him, she felt very privileged. A young, vulnerable wild animal was placing his trust in her. She couldn't help smiling. It was wonderful. Once the bottle was drained, she left the pen.

'I know it's tempting to stay and play and cuddle him,' said Ade. 'But it's best that you don't. We want him to reintegrate

with his own kind and the longer he spends
with humans, the harder that will be.'

'I understand,' said Tilly.

'Well, that's it for now. Go and enjoy
yourself at the spring. I'm sure Sekongo
will drive you up to the reserve for a visit
before you leave.'

'Thanks,' she said.

She knew the vet was right, but as she looked back at Stripy she wished she could play with him all night and day.

Just then, she saw a group of people coming towards the pen. Peter Melesi was with them. It was the team from the game reserve.

'Time to say goodbye,' said Ade.

'Can I stroke him?' said Tilly.

'I guess once won't hurt.'

Tilly ran her hand down Stripy's forehead and nose.

'I'll miss you,' she said. 'But I know you'll be very happy where you're going. And I've got to get back to my own horse, Magic Spirit. He was a rescue horse, just like you.'

The little zebra lowered his head. Tilly patted his shoulder. She smoothed her hand along his mane and along his tail. His hairs were short and stubby. The stray ones came away in her hands and she realised she could make a bracelet out of them – one that she would keep for herself, to remember him by.

She stepped back.

'Come on,' said Brook, squeezing her shoulder. 'Let's go swimming!'

Tilly and Brook found Mrs Redbrow at the spring. They didn't waste a moment and both dived into the water. It was very refreshing. After splashing around, swimming, and practising underwater diving, they lay on the grassy bank and watched the sun set.

'This is the life,' said Brook. 'I've almost completely forgotten about exams. I wonder how Solo's doing. The stable-hands at Cavendish Hall are looking after him and they're very experienced, but I can't help worrying.'

'I know,' said Tilly. 'I keep thinking about Magic too.'

'You two sound like anxious parents!' said Tilly's mum. 'Now you know how it feels when we worry about you!'

Tilly grinned and rolled her eyes, but after caring for Stripy, she understood what her mum meant. She felt very protective. He was so tiny and dependant on people to feed him and keep him safe.

That evening, Tilly, her mum, and Brook ate at a big table in the open air with the other guests. They had a delicious stew made from ostrich meat, followed by an African fruit salad.

Then they went back to their tent and played cards to the sound of crickets and monkey howls. The night was amazing, and so clear. Tilly couldn't believe how many stars she could see.

'I hope Stripy's okay,' said Tilly. 'I guess he's arrived at his new reserve now.'

'He'll be all right once he's with his new herd,' said Brook reassuringly.

'You're right,' she said. 'The vet said Sekongo might take us to visit him. I don't want to leave Botswana without seeing him one more time.'

Nine

Over the next few days they did more
riding. Sekongo took them to his favourite
places, including an idyllic water hole.
They saw hippos, giraffes and many more
zebras. And sure enough, on the last day
of their trip, Sekongo offered to drive
Tilly, Brook and Tilly's mum to the game
reserve. The trip took several hours. By
midday the sun was beating down.

'Phew! It's hot!' said Tilly's mum.

'Not far now,' said Sekongo. 'In fact, all

this land over here is part of the reserve.'

He pointed across the bush.

'Wow!' said Tilly. 'It must be huge.'

'Yes, plenty of room for the animals to roam free.'

Eventually they came to a large set of gates, with a sign welcoming them. They turned onto a track, and in the distance Tilly could see a compound of buildings.

'That's the hotel and guest lodges,' said Sekongo. 'It has five stars. Very grand.'

'How about that?' said Brook. 'A luxury new home for Stripy!'

'I think Stripy would be just as happy with a bit of grass and some trees,' said Tilly.

As they pulled up by the reception building, Peter Melesi was waiting for them.

'Dumela!' he said. 'Welcome!'

He shook Sekongo's hand, then greeted Tilly and the others.

'How's Stripy?' said Tilly eagerly.

'He's very good. We have a well-established zebra herd here,' Peter explained. 'And we're doing everything we can to make sure Stripy is accepted. We regularly take abandoned animals and reintegrate them into wilds of the reserve, so we know our stuff.'

Tilly smiled. It was good to hear such encouraging things.

'You've had a long journey. Why don't you get some refreshments, then I'll get one of our team to give you a tour.'

Tilly, her mum, Brook and Sekongo went to the reception where they were given some delicious fruit juice. They were met by a young African woman, who was wearing a khaki safari suit.

'I hear you would like to have a look round the reserve. My name is Iniko. I'm going to be your guide.'

'Sounds great,' said Tilly's mum, taking a last mouthful of juice.

They followed Iniko back outside.

'You must be Tilly,' Iniko said, as she led them to an off-road buggy decorated with the game reserve's logo. 'Peter told me he met you on a horse safari. Are you a keen rider?'

'Yes,' said Tilly. 'I ride a grey called Magic Spirit at my stables. I helped rescue him when he was abandoned by a roadside.'

'So, you're used to rescuing animals. No wonder you've been so good with Stripy. Maybe it's your destiny. To help troubled animals.'

Tilly smiled. It was true. She did have an instinct for helping horses. There'd been others before Stripy. She thought of

Goliath, the huge draught horse, and how she'd helped the World Horse Welfare team with him. He was now fit and healthy and training to be a drum horse. She thought of Red Admiral. And Samson. And Pride and Joy.

And, of course, Magic Spirit.

Finding Magic had changed her life as well as his. It had led to the start of her visits to Silver Shoe Farm, which was like a second home to her now.

'I expect you're looking forward to seeing your horse again,' said Iniko.

'Oh, yes,' said Tilly, missing him suddenly.

It wasn't long now. She couldn't wait to tell him about Stripy.

'Does everyone drive around in these?' said Tilly's mum, as she climbed into the buggy.

'The reserve is so vast,' said Iniko. 'It would take days to walk from one side to the other, plus the buggy gives us protection. You have to remember, although the animals are carefully monitored, they're still wild. We're entering their world and we have to respect their ways.'

She started the engine and the buggy pulled away. It wasn't long before the buildings of the hotel and reception were small specks on the horizon. They bounced down a dirt track and entered a dense area of trees. Along the way, Iniko talked about

how many animals they had at the reserve, how many different species.

They saw giraffes, and different types of antelope. Eventually they stopped at a large watering hole. It was a blanket of pink.

'Flamingos!' Tilly's mum exclaimed. 'Aren't they beautiful?'

Suddenly, there was a flurry of activity. Some of the flamingos fluffed their wings 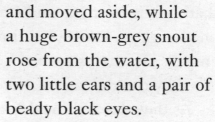 and moved aside, while a huge brown-grey snout rose from the water, with two little ears and a pair of beady black eyes.

'Is that a hippo?' said Tilly.

'Yes. His name is Obadiah. This is his spot. We always find him here at this time of day, cooling off in the muddy water.'

'Do all your animals have names?' asked Brook.

Iniko laughed.

'No. There are hundreds of different beasts, big and small, within the reserve. The ones that get names are the ones who, for various reasons, need special monitoring, medical treatment, or become part of our breeding programme. Or sometimes they simply have big personalities!'

'What about Stripy?' said Tilly.

'Since he's already been named, I guess that's going to stick. And I'm sure he'll be one we get to know over time. The rescue animals are always special.'

Tilly couldn't agree more.

As they drove through a cluster of trees, a herd of zebras came into view. And suddenly, there was Stripy. Tilly recognised him immediately, those wobbly legs and big black eyes.

'He looks so happy,' she said.

Iniko stopped the buggy. The herd passed in front of it. Most of the zebras kept their distance, but Stripy came up close. He tipped his head to one side and shook his mane.

'Do you think he recognises us?' said Brook.

'It's possible,' said Iniko. 'After all, you helped save his life.'

Tilly smiled to herself as they watched the zebra herd move away. It really had been the most wonderful holiday. She couldn't wait to tell Magic all about it.

Ten

On the flight home, Tilly made her zebra-hair bracelet. She imagined returning to the game reserve one day and being greeted by Stripy. She pictured him as a fully-grown zebra male with bold black stripes, but with that same sweet look in his eyes.

She daydreamed about it all the way back to the UK, though as the plane landed, her thoughts were firmly with Silver Shoe Farm.

'Can we go straight there, please?' she begged her mum.

'I could do with a rest before I go anywhere. It's so early in the morning. Aren't you jetlagged?'

But there was no point arguing. Tilly's mum knew Tilly too well.

'We'll see if your dad will take you,' she said, smiling.

Tilly's dad was happy to drive her to Silver Shoe. As soon as they pulled into the tree-lined lane and she saw the familiar cluster of white farm buildings, Tilly sighed with joy. Even though it was cold, the sky was bright and the sun was shining.

They drove through the gate and parked in the yard. Tilly stepped out of the car and took a deep breath. She loved the smell of fresh hay, and today it seemed especially welcoming.

Mia, Angela and Duncan rushed over to say hello.

'You're back! How was it?'

'You've got a sun tan!'

'Which animals did you see?'

They all talked at once. Tilly grinned.

'I had an amazing encounter,' she said. 'With a little zebra foal called Stripy.'

'Wow!' said Mia. 'I want to hear all about that.'

But before Tilly could tell the story properly, she wanted to see Magic.

'How's he been?'

'Absolutely fine,' said Angela. 'He's down in the long field. He'll be delighted to see you.'

Tilly's dad stayed to talk to Angela and Duncan, while Mia and Tilly went down to the field. Tilly's heart began to beat fast at the thought of seeing Magic again.

'I've missed him so much,' she said.

When Magic saw her, there was no doubt he had missed Tilly too. He pricked his ears and galloped towards the gate.

He shook his head and quivered with happiness. She threw her arms around his neck and gave him a kiss.

'Hello, boy,' she cooed, reaching up to stroke him.

Magic's eyes were bright and his coat was glossy. He'd obviously been well cared for, although she'd never doubted that Mia, Angela and Duncan would do a great job.

'Thanks,' she said to Mia. 'He looks really happy and content.'

Tilly reached her arm up to tickle his ears, and her sleeve fell back.

'You've got a new bracelet,' Mia said, admiring the plaited zebra hairs around Tilly's wrist. Magic prodded it with his nose.

'It's from Stripy,' said Tilly.

'Tell us more,' said Mia. 'What was he like?'

'He was adorable! He was just like a horse foal, like Lucky Chance, but . . . different somehow. I got to feed him with a bottle.'

'Aw,' said Mia. 'That's so cute!'

'I'd love to go back and see him again
one day,' said Tilly. 'When he's fully
grown. He's being rehabilitated with a new
zebra herd on a game reserve.'

Magic lifted his head and snorted.

'Are you listening, Magic? I promised
Stripy I'd tell you all about him!'

Mia laughed.

'No wonder you and Magic are so close. You talk to him about everything, don't you?'

'Of course,' said Tilly. 'He's my best friend – my best horse friend, I mean.'

Then she looked at Mia and gave her a hug.

'It's good to be back,' she said. 'I've missed you too.'

Mia glanced at her watch.

'I'd better go,' she said. 'My mum's picking me up in five minutes. She's taking me shopping to get some new jodhpur boots. Come along if you like?'

'Thanks,' said Tilly. 'But I might just stay with Magic for a while. I'll see you later.'

Mia returned to the yard, leaving Tilly and Magic alone. They stood together, she on one side of the fence, him on the other, but feeling as close as any horse and rider could. As Tilly rested her head against Magic's shoulder, she felt him nose Stripy's bracelet again.

'Maybe Iniko was right,' she whispered.
'Maybe it is my destiny to rescue horses.
I know I have a special bond with you,
Magic, because I spend most of my time
with you. But with Stripy, the bond seemed
to come from nowhere. It was so strange,
but amazing.'

Magic twitched his ears and nuzzled her
neck.

'Perhaps it's because, in a way, you're
both like me,' said Tilly thoughtfully.
'All three of us have had to be rescued. I
was rescued by the Redbrows when they
adopted me. And I guess I was also rescued
by Silver Shoe Farm, because coming here
has allowed me to do what I love best. You,
me and Stripy, we understand each other,
don't we?'

She looked into Magic's eyes, then
gazed up at the sky.

It seemed so big and blue, not quite
as big as the African sky, but big enough
to make her wonder where her love of
horses would take her next. She patted

Magic once more and felt the warmth of
his breath on her hands. Then he rested
his head on her shoulder and gave a quiet,
contented nicker.

Pippa's Top Tips
for Safari

Whenever you go away on holiday, make sure there is someone responsible taking care of your horse or pony.

Be honest about your riding ability. Most horseback safaris cater for varying levels of riding – they'll assess your level and match you with the best horse.

June to August is the best time to visit Botswana. It's their winter, but it's also the dry season, so the weather conditions are excellent for seeing all sorts of wildlife.

It can be chilly in the morning and evenings so don't forget to pack warm clothes.

The Okavango Delta has been described as a 'water meadow', and between May and December many of the flood plains are full. The horses have to wade from island to island – so be prepared to get a bit wet!

As well as your usual riding gear, take a wide brimmed hat and long-sleeved cotton tops to cover your shoulders.

Make sure your riding clothes are in neutral colours – khaki or bush colours – no red or white if possible.

Remember to take plenty of sun cream. Horseback safari is great fun, but it's hard work too – so don't overestimate your stamina, and if you need a break from the trekking, don't be afraid to relax at the camp.

Every safari has an element of danger – that's what makes it exciting. But wild animals are unpredictable, so it's important to stay alert, to listen to your guide and follow instructions at all times.

Enjoy it! This is a once in a lifetime opportunity to see all sorts of different animals, including elephants, buffalo, giraffes, wildebeests, monkeys, lions, cheetahs, wild dogs – and, of course, zebras!

Glossary

Thoroughbred (p.10) – Tall, slim, athletic horse used in racing and other equestrian sports.

Grooming (p.17) – Regular grooming cleans your horse and will prevent any chafing under tack. It keeps your horse healthy and comfortable and will help you form a relationship with him.

Hack (p.26) – Riding in the country for pleasure.

Game ride (p.40) – Wildlife spotting on horseback.

Game reserve (p.48) – An area of land set aside for conservation purposes, where wildlife live in their natural habitat and ecosystems are protected. Many game reserves are in Africa, where they are home to rhinoceros, elephant, buffalo, leopard and lion.

White snip and socks (p.49) – a snip is a white marking on a horse's muzzle, and a sock is a white marking on a horse's leg which extends higher than the fetlock but not as high as the knee.

hh / hands high (p.49) – Horses and ponies are measured in 'hands', a hand is 4 inches or 10.16 cm.

Buckskin (p.50) – A hair coat colour of horses, consisting of a tan or gold coat with black markings on the mane, tail and lower legs.

Mucking out (p.51) – Your horse or pony's stable needs mucking out once or twice a day, to remove droppings and wet bedding and then replace with fresh bedding.

Draught horse (p.89) – A large horse bred for hard, heavy tasks such as ploughing and farm labour. Draught horses tend to be strong and patient with a docile temperament.

World Horse Welfare (p.89) – A charity dedicated to giving abused and neglected horses a second chance in life by rescuing and re-homing them. In the UK, World Horse Welfare have four farms open to visitors where many of their 2,000 horses are kept. Visit www.worldhorsewelfare.org for more information.

Points of a Horse

1. poll
2. ear
3. eye
4. mane
5. crest
6. withers
7. back
8. loins
9. croup
10. dock
11. flank
12. tail
13. tendons
14. hock joint
15. stomach

16. elbow
17. heel
18. hoof
19. coronet band
20. pastern
21. fetlock joint
22. cannon bone
23. knee
24. shoulder
25. chin groove
26. nostril
27. muzzle
28. nose
29. cheekbone
30. forelock

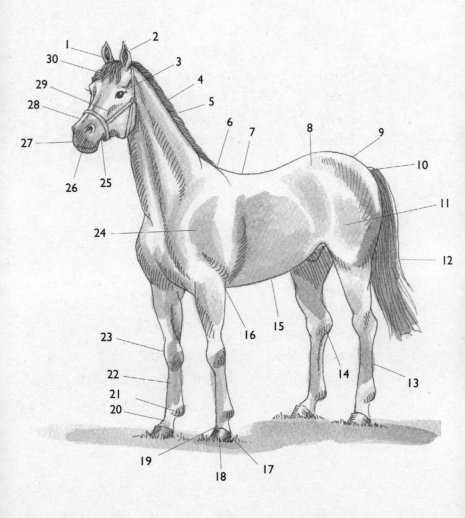

111

Pippa Funnell

"Winning is amazing for a minute, but then I am striving again to reach my next goal."

I began learning to ride when I was six, on a little pony called Pepsi.

When I was seven, I joined my local Pony Club – the perfect place to learn more about riding and caring for horses.

By the time I was fourteen and riding my first horse, Sir Barnaby, my dream of being an event rider was starting to take shape.

Two years later, I was offered the opportunity to train as a working pupil in Norfolk with Ruth McMullen, the legendary riding teacher. I jumped at the chance.

In 1987, Sir Barnaby and I won the individual gold together at the Young Rider European Championships, which was held in Poland.

Since then, hard work and determination have taken me all the way to the biggest eventing competitions in the world. I've been lucky and had success at major events like Bramham, Burghley, Badminton, Luhmühlen, Le Lion d'Angers, Hickstead, Blenheim, Windsor, Saumur, Pau, Kentucky – and the list goes on…

I married William Funnell in 1993. William is an international show jumper and horse breeder. He has helped me enormously with my show jumping. We live on a farm in the beautiful Surrey countryside – with lots of stables!

Every sportsman or woman's wildest dream is to be asked to represent their country at the Olympics. So in 2000, when I was chosen for the Sydney Olympics, I was delighted. It was even more special to be part of the silver medal winning team.

Then, in 2003, I became the first (and only) person to win eventing's most coveted prize – the Rolex Grand Slam. The Grand Slam (winning three of the big events in a row – Badminton, Kentucky and Burghley) is the only three-day eventing slam in the sporting world.

2004 saw another Olympics and another call-up. Team GB performed brilliantly again and won another well-deserved silver medal, and I was lucky enough to win an individual bronze.

Having had several years without any top horses, I spent my time producing youngsters, so it was great in 2010 when one of those came through – Redesigned, a handsome chestnut gelding. In June that year I won my third Bramham International Horse Trials title on Redesigned. We even managed a clear show jumping round in the pouring rain! By the end of 2010, Redesigned was on the squad for the World Championships in Kentucky where we finished fifth.

Today, as well as a hectic competition schedule, I'm also busy training horses for the future. At the Billy Stud, I work with my husband, William, and top breeder, Donal Barnwell, to produce top-class sport horses.

And in between all that I love writing the *Tilly's Pony Tails* books, and I'm also a trustee of World Horse Welfare, a fantastic charity dedicated to giving abused and neglected horses a second chance in life. For more information, visit their website at www.worldhorsewelfare.org.

Acknowledgements

Three years ago when my autobiography was published I never imagined that I would find myself writing children's books. Huge thanks go to Louisa Leaman for helping me to bring Tilly to life, and to Jennifer Miles for her wonderful illustrations.

Many thanks to Fiona Kennedy for persuading and encouraging me to search my imagination and for all her hard work, along with the rest of the team at Orion. Due to my riding commitments I am not the easiest person to get hold of as my agent Jonathan Marks at MTC has found. It's a relief he has been able to work on all the agreements for me.

Much of my thinking about Tilly has been done out loud in front of family, friends and godchildren – thank you all for listening.

More than anything I have to acknowledge my four-legged friends – my horses. It is thanks to them, and the great moments I have had with them, that I was able to create a girl, Tilly, who like me follows her passions.

Pippa Funnell
Forest Green, February 2009

For more about Tilly and
Silver Shoe Farm – including pony tips,
quizzes and everything you ever wanted
to know about horses –
visit www.tillysponytails.co.uk

Look out for

Pippa Funnell: Follow Your Dreams

Pippa Funnell as you've never seen her before.

Get to know Pippa – her loves, her hates, her friends, her family. Meet her beautiful horses, and take a sneaky peek at life on her gorgeous farm. Find out how she prepares for important competitions, trains and cares for her horses, and still has the time to write *Tilly's Pony Tails*.

And discover how, with hard work, passion and determination, you too can follow your dreams, just like Pippa.

978 1 4440 0266 9

£6.99

the orion star

Sign up for **the orion star** newsletter to get inside information about your favourite children's authors as well as exclusive competitions and early reading copy giveaways.

www.orionbooks.co.uk/newsletters

Follow  on **twitter**

Orion
Children's Books